Yet Life

Yet Life

Rajesh Chatterjee

Translated by
Dr. Chandrajyoti Sen Majumder

EXCELLER BOOKS®
A GLOBAL PRESS

Yet Life

Cover by Exceller Books
Translated by Dr. Chandrajyoti Sen Majumder

ISBN: 978-93-47397-18-9

Published in India in 2025 by Exceller Books,
An imprint of GE Group,
G1, Dream Apartment, Degree College Road, Belgharia,
Kolkata, 700056, India
www.excellerbooks.com

EXCELLER BOOKS®
A GLOBAL PRESS

To the person to whom I have dedicated all my writings, not just this book—To Tilottama!

Contents

Chapter 1

The clock had just ticked past seven, and Raktim dragged himself out of bed against his will. It was going to be a special day, so he could not afford to waste any time and finished his chores in the washroom first. In the next twenty minutes, he rushed through everything to make sure he reached the breakfast table on time.

Meanwhile, the newspaper man, Tapas uncle, had delivered the newspaper, and Raktim's father, Biswanath Babu, continued to study the morning headlines through his specs.

"*Ma*, please give me something to eat quickly. A car is coming to pick me up soon."

While rushing back to his room, the thought of Tapas uncle struck Raktim; the man's devotion to his monotonous routine was surprising. Raktim wondered how someone could, day after day, pedal around such an uneventful mufassil town like theirs, delivering newspapers and magazines, yet never seem to protest against the boredom of life. Raktim had noticed that not only he but also his father liked Tapas uncle.

He quickly packed his small bag and hurriedly finished his breakfast. Then, while he was washing his hands, Malati, his mother, asked, "How many days of leave have you taken from your school job?"

"Don't worry, *Ma*. I'll be back tonight, so I've applied for just one day of casual leave for tomorrow."

Raktim rushed to his room to finish the last-minute chores before leaving. Suddenly, he remembered to call Raqib, who was a late riser. If he arrived late, their journey from Suri to the Kolkata Book Fair would be jeopardized, and that would spoil Raktim's plan to meet his favourite author, Shyamali di, there.

"Good morning, *bhaijan*!"

"Good morning, brother! Where are you now?"

"I'm still at home, but I'm leaving soon."

"Hurry up, or we'll be late."

"Let me just finish my tiffin. I'm coming."

"Hmm. Fine."

Raktim put down the phone and thought of Vincent Smith's line, "Unity in Diversity." He smiled to himself. This lad, Raqib, had driven cars in Mumbai for six years, but during the pandemic, he was forced to return to Suri. Then slowly, with his own savings and some borrowings, he bought a Maruti car and started renting it out locally. Although he had settled back, he was still struggling with the culture and lifestyle of this suburban Bengali locality.

The car arrived soon and honked at least four times. Raktim tied his shoelaces and got ready to leave. He slung the red bag over his shoulder — the one he had recently bought from the *Poush Mela* in Shantiniketan.

"The car has arrived. I'm leaving."

Raktim did not like the idea of wearing a seatbelt over his freshly ironed shirt, so he chose to sit in the back seat. Raqib started the engine and drove off, only to stop again just a kilometer later. Raktim cursed his luck as he looked at the scene ahead.

Chapter 2

A month ago, a meme was trending on social media that joked, 'People of Suri love licking lollipops.' Raktim had seen it on Facebook while scrolling through his news feed. Now, he remembered it even more clearly, because right in front of him was the same problem that commuters here face every day — the railway gate at Hutton Bazar was closed. Reaching Karunamoyee was definitely going to take a long time now.

"Raqib, you'll have to drive faster now."

"Sure, *bhaijan*! Don't worry — I'll make sure you arrive on time."

Raqib kept chewing his usual amount of gutka. Feeling irritated, Raktim took out his phone and began scrolling through his Facebook news feed. He noticed that Shyamali di had posted an update just twelve minutes ago. She had written, "I'll be at the Bodhibriksh stall with my poetry book *Diotima* around two in the afternoon. The stall number is 333. Let's catch up, friends!"

Raktim gave a love reaction to the post and commented, "I'm coming, didi. Do give me an autograph."

As he slipped his phone back into his pocket, Raktim realized that by that time, he would only make it as far as Bolpur. He leaned back in the seat and closed his eyes, hoping for a moment of peace. But instead, memories from his past rushed into the darkness behind his eyelids. His life had seen so many ups and downs that he had long lost count. Many events were now buried in the shadows of time.

One such memory went back to when he was only four years old. He had been admitted to a nursing home in Kolkata due to breathing problems, and one night, child traffickers had almost kidnapped him from there. The alert Kolkata Police had stopped the attempt just in time, saving his life. Ever since that incident, Raktim carried a quiet fear of Kolkata—one that he never shared with anyone.

A message notification chimed on his phone, pulling Raktim out of his thoughts. He checked the screen and saw that the WhatsApp message was from Rohit. Rohit lived in Naktala and ran a public relations agency. He also managed an NGO called *Prayas* and served on the editorial board of a weekly magazine named *Astha*.

Raktim's own poetry book, a four-format collection titled *Kheyali Kham* (meaning *Envelope of Whims*), was set to be published at this year's Kolkata Book Fair. To help promote it on social media and reach more readers, he had transferred about three thousand rupees to Rohit. Now, Rohit had sent him a sample of the promotional video and after seeing it Raktim was both happy and impressed. For a moment, he felt confident that one day he would be loved and respected by thousands. But then, the helpless face of the elderly poet Binay Majumdar suddenly came to his mind.

Chapter 3

The Book Fair opened at noon, so Raktim did not have enough time to snack properly at Shaktigarh before rushing ahead. Even then, by the time he arrived, it was already half past one. He asked Raqib to wait with the car in the parking area and walked alone past the Karunamoyee Bus Stand toward the designated stall.

Just then, he noticed a pair of kohl-smeared eyes of a girl.

Amidst the jostling crowd at the Book Fair, her masked face was turned upward, staring blankly at the autumn sky. Nearby, a tea seller was handing out cups of lemon tea to people sitting around her. Some book lovers were strolling about, chatting casually while sipping their tea. But the girl stood still, lost in her own world.

The bustling crowd did not allow Raktim to stop and look at her for long. Pushed and swept forward, he regretted not being able to see her face beneath the mask. Those eyes had already captured his heart, and he could only imagine how beautiful she must be.

When Raktim finally reached the stall of *Annya Manan,* he found a decent crowd already gathered there. Books were being sold, and the atmosphere was lively. Noticing him arrive, the publisher, Debayan Saha, warmly handed over the thirty author copies that had been set aside for Raktim.

Raktim quickly said, "No, please don't give me all the copies right now. Just hand me ten for the moment. You can courier the rest to my home whenever it's convenient."

He slipped the ten copies of *Kheyali Kham* into his bag and hurried toward stall number 333. It was already ten past two, which meant Shyamali di must have reached the Bodhibriksha stall by then. Raktim did not want to be late.

When he reached the Bodhibriksha stall, Raktim found exactly what he had expected—Shyamali di was already there, happily chatting with fellow poets and authors. Her book *Diotima* was neatly stacked on the stall's table along with other titles.

At first, she didn't notice him in the crowd. So, Raktim stepped closer and gently whispered, "Didi, I'm here."

Shyamali di looked pleasantly surprised. "Oh wow! What a lovely surprise! When did you arrive, Raktim?"

"I came about half an hour ago," he replied. "Please give me a copy of *Diotima*. I'd like to buy one."

Raktim always believed that relationships are priceless. Writing poetry brought him closer to many people he would never have met otherwise. He became an older brother to some and a younger one to others. Without the courage to enter the literary world, he knew his life would have missed the warmth of these wonderful connections.

He walked up to the front desk of the Bodhibriksha stall, where Shyamali di's latest literary work, *Diotima*, was beautifully displayed. After purchasing a copy, he returned to her and said with a smile, "Didi, please put an autograph on this book for me."

With a warm smile, Shyamali di signed the book and wrote lovingly, *"To Raktim, with loads of good wishes."* She dated her signature as 6th March 2022. Then, all of a sudden, she raised her voice and called out, "Tilottama, come here for a moment! Do you know Raktim? He's a talented writer from Suri."

Raktim sensed that the woman she was speaking to was standing right behind him. He turned around—only to witness something he was completely unprepared for.

Chapter 4

Afamous dialogue from the film *Om Shanti Om* had become widely popular, and like many others, it had captured Raktim's attention too. He would often quote it among his school friends. The line is: "The picture is yet to reach its climax, pal." When Shyamali di spoke, those words flashed in his mind again—just as he turned to witness a scene he could never have imagined.

Tilottama, the woman being welcomed, was the same kohl-eyed girl who had stolen his heart only minutes before. Now she stood without her mask, revealing lips so strikingly red that they seemed capable of setting him ablaze with the slightest provocation. Raktim thought — *Uff, this is why truth is stranger than fiction.*

Still dazed, he walked up to Tilottama and extended his hand. "Nice to meet you," he said. She simply smiled back, silently acknowledging the moment.

Still trying to overcome his daze, Raktim felt he should look away before anyone noticed his flustered state. He quickly pretended to search his bag for the poetry book he wanted to gift Shyamali di. But the growing crowd inside the stall made it difficult, so he asked, "Didi, could you please hold my bag for a moment?"

Before Shyamali di could respond, Tilottama jumped in playfully, "Hey, even I can hold it!"

Her words sparked a thought in him. Instead of one, he pulled out two copies of the poetry book—one for Shyamali di and one for Tilottama. He handed them over and attempted to leave the stall as fast as he could. But just as he turned to go, Shyamali di asked the boy at the cash counter to take a few pictures of them together. "Please take some photos of us on my phone," she requested. The boy agreed, and after a couple of quick smiles for the camera, Raktim thanked her and stepped out.

There was a surprising lightness in his chest. He had clearly noticed how Tilottama had moved out of the frame when the photos were taken—almost as if she did not want to intrude.

The Book Fair crowd now felt suffocating for Raktim, and despite being surrounded by people, he felt strangely alone. So, he headed to the Karunamoyee bus stand, lit a cigarette, checked his phone for network, and called Raqib to let him know it was time to leave.

Yet, as he exhaled the smoke into the air, one sentence kept echoing inside him: *"Even I can hold… Even I can… Even I can…"*

Chapter 5

Raktim's grandmother always used to say that any dream seen at dawn is bound to come true. She had passed away from old age shortly before the COVID pandemic hit in 2020. Since then, only Raktim and his parents have been living in the house. After leaving the Book Fair and having some light refreshments, Raktim finally set off from Kolkata to Suri. By the time he reached home, it was already dawn. Exhausted, he went straight to bed; sleep overwhelming him like a tidal wave. And just then, after so many years, his grandmother's words came back to him.

Raktim was a primary school teacher. Although his school was open that day—Monday, 7th March—he had already taken a casual leave. When he finally woke up, the clock showed a quarter past eleven. He could not help but laugh. It was not dawn, and he had not dreamed of anything. He vaguely remembered reading somewhere that people forget most of their dreams, and that dreams do not come during deep sleep but in the lighter stages. After the long journey and hours of walking around the fair, he was completely exhausted and slept soundly. So, there was no chance of dreaming about Tilottama.

But that did not rob him of the real memory of what had happened at the book fair the previous day. After freshening up and having breakfast, Raktim returned to his study room and stood before his table. He looked at the calendar and quietly marked the date—6th March—with a red pen, enclosing the number as if sealing a promise: "We will meet again, Tilottama. Surely, we will."

Chapter 6

There was a journal called *Literature Today*, edited by Shyamali di. It had been published regularly for the past three years, featuring works by many well-known poets and writers. The journal also had a Facebook group, which was frequently updated with information about upcoming issues and the new authors whose works were being featured.

With hopeful anticipation, Raktim opened the page. He soon found a collection of photos from yesterday's gathering in front of the Bodhibriksha stall. The people in the photos had been tagged, and to his delight, he found himself tagged in a few of them. He began carefully going through the names, and one particular name made his heart race—*Tilottama Mukhopadhyay*. Without hesitation, he sent her a friend request.

And then? Well, he told himself that now he must wait—because waiting, too, has its own thrill. For different people and at different times in life, the excitement of waiting varies. To Raktim, waiting was like the journey of a river, like the passage of time itself.

Trying to distract himself, he looked at the pile of books beside him. There were many close friends he wanted to gift his poetry book to—people who had stood by him since his earliest days as a writer. He counted seven such names, certain they would remain with him till the end.

Next, he phoned his college friend, Lisa, who worked as an officer in the cybercrime department in Suri, handling cases of fraud and online criminal activities around the world. The moment she picked up, she teased him warmly, "Wow! So the famous poet Raktim Chatterjee finally finds time to call! A great man indeed—someone whose book gets published at the Kolkata Book Fair! Do visit us once you're free!"

"Oh, stop it! Enough teasing," Raktim laughed. "I want to gift you a copy of my poetry book. Tell me when it would be convenient for me to visit."

"No need to worry about that," she replied. "I'll come by some Sunday and collect my gift. And by the way, I love the title—*Khamkheyali,* meaning whims—I saw it on Facebook!"

"Uff, you didn't see it properly! The name is *Kheyali Kham*—the envelope of whims."

"Ah, yes, *Kheyali Kham*! My mistake," she chuckled. "Alright, I'm in the middle of something. We'll talk later. Keep writing! Bye!"

"Thanks, dear. Bye," he said, smiling.

He lay back, intending to rest a bit, when a Facebook notification suddenly popped up—Tilottama Mukhopadhyay had accepted his friend request. Uff! Dear life, what more could one ask for?

Chapter 7

Raktim argued with himself that he needed to be stricter with his life—organize it and put its scattered pieces together. Life was short, and he had to act fast.

A few months earlier, he had visited Durgapur Junction Mall with his father, Biswanath Babu. There, he took a picture beside a statue of a sad-faced clown, which he had set as his Facebook DP. Now, he felt like changing it. He chose an old photograph from his phone—one where he was holding Rabindranath Tagore's *Jiban Smriti*. The picture had been forgotten in his gallery, but suddenly felt meaningful again. Tagore's works, he believed, reveal new depths in different stages of life. Not only that, but the bard's countless Rabindra Sangeet possess that timeless magic. Secretly, Raktim wished that after his death, someone would place a *Gitabitan* instead of the *Gita* beside him.

While scrolling through Tilottama's Facebook profile, something caught his eye—her relationship status: *Single.* He immediately thanked his fortune. In such moments, he felt like believing in God, though the unrest in the world often turned him away from faith. But he considered his changing moods natural—just a part of living in this complex world.

Then, another thought struck him: after everything that had happened, what had he truly gained? He noticed some beautiful poems on Tilottama's timeline and read them all before going to bed. Being impressed, he could not help but send a message to Tilottama over the messenger, which read: *"You are an awesome writer. Keep up the great work. Your thoughts are really on a different level."*

To his surprise, she read the message instantly. A green dot lit up beside her DP, and he saw the three dots—she was typing.

"And I'll share my reviews with you soon."

"Reviews? What reviews?"

"Your poems—the ones you gifted me."

"Oh, that. No rush. But there's something I must tell you. I felt really bad about one thing that day."

"What is it?"

"The photographer... he should have captured the full frame."

"I see."

"You stepped aside, and I didn't want you to leave the picture. But I couldn't call you back in front of everyone, thinking it might feel awkward."

"Don't worry. That was unintentional. And as long as we're alive, there will always be chances to take more pictures together."

"Thank you. I feel much better after sharing my thoughts."

"Now let me share something small with you. Keep it if you like."

She sent him a link to a poetry reading group called *Poems from a Different Autumn*. Underneath it read: *"You don't need to do anything. Just take a look if you like."*

Raktim immediately joined the group and said, "Okay, I joined."

The next message that floated on his mobile screen said, "Keep a headphone if you want."

"Should I tell others? Maybe invite people here?"

"No need. This is just for passion. Stay here, enjoy first. Don't crowd the place unnecessarily."

"I promise to dedicate my next poetry book to you. You can even take a screenshot of today's chat if you want."

"I trust you, but I won't give you false praise. I'll analyze every poem. Poetry is emotional—one must handle it with care. I'm just an ordinary poetry lover trying my best."

"I'm so glad to know you. Tell me—are you as emotional as your poems?"

"Pleasure is mine, dear. I'm equally surprised to find an autumnal barbet singing at my doorstep. Anyway, I'm not a big intellectual with too many emotions."

"Really?"

"It's hard to say. Okay then, let's stop here for today. I have to wake up early in the morning for the office."

"Good night, sweet dreams."

Raktim lay still for a long time, lost in her words, until the ticking clock pulled him back to reality. Wrapped in his blanket, he kept thinking about her. She used ellipses—those three dots—everywhere. Raktim wished he could become one of those dots in her life. But ellipses always had three dots. If he was one, who were the other two? Was there someone else?

Chapter 8

The world was celebrating International Women's Day, and Raktim took the opportunity to wish the woman who had, in those days, won the most important place in his heart. Tilottama replied with a "Thanks" within the next half hour, shortening Raktim's wait. He promptly wrote back, "You're welcome."

He messaged her again that night. His desire to talk to her was becoming irresistible. He had lost control of himself and was constantly looking for opportunities to reach out. For example, as soon as he saw her online, he sent a message: "I have a request for a poem from you. I'm planning to publish it in my magazine. It will likely be published early next year."

"Wow, what is your magazine called?"

"Stories of poetry. The magazine goes by this name."

"That's a nice name."

A few minutes later, a poem arrived from Tilottama along with a comment: "You know, poems are generally girly by nature, so they never have a shortage of stories."

"I agree with your views. I must admit, you have a rational approach to almost everything in life. It's a wonderful side of you."

"Thinking drives poems, doesn't it?"

"I like your style of writing. It's quite unusual. Most poets don't write like you. I can feel that you write from your heart."

"Nah! What I've written so far is just a tiny part of my feelings. But the more I write, the more I feel the lines will ultimately hurt the heart of my poem. Poems are very soft-hearted, you know."

"Believe me, your unique poems have already touched my heart. They will take you a long way in the world of poetry — mark my words."

Tilottama sent a new poem. It was called *Arohan*, or 'ascend.'

"The poem was published last month in the *Shatadal* magazine," she wrote.

Raktim knew about *Shatadal*; it was a renowned journal. The poem was equally brilliant.

Raktim promptly wrote, "Brilliant poem. Please assure me that you will also give a poem to my magazine. Undoubtedly, that will uphold my magazine's honor."

"Your high praises are making me blush. I promise I'll give you a poem for your magazine — but stop praising me, will you?"

"Okay. By the way, I'm looking forward to your birthday. I'll definitely call right at midnight to wish you."

"Can you tell me what else you do for a living?"

"Rather, tell me something about yourself. We can keep my side of the story for our next session instead."

"What would you expect about me beyond what you've already seen?"

"Well, I don't know you very well yet, but from what I've understood so far, you're a very honest person with a golden heart."

"You're better off in a way, since you can already form an opinion about me. I barely know anything about you. But I believe writing can bridge that gap in understanding. Maybe one day you'll realize I'm not the person you think I am."

"I'm sure I'm not mistaken." Raktim wrote but felt sheepish on the contrary, as Tilottama perhaps joked while writing the reply, "So you're claiming that you understood me in just a meeting that only lasted a few minutes. That's quite a skill then!"

Raktim reasoned, "Well, at least give me a chance to explain the reason behind my claim."

"Sure, go ahead."

"When in the stall, I was facing a problem in handling the heavy bag full of books in the middle of the crowded stall; you were the one who came to help. Your gesture was so touching."

"Oh my! But that's a pretty common gesture."

"I find you very open-minded when you talk. You write well, yet you never boast about it, and that impresses me. You always have a reason behind everything you say, which is also remarkable. But more than anything, I'm impressed by your behavior. Hardly anyone treats unfamiliar people the way you do."

"Stop. Otherwise, the way you're going on with your explanation, you'll end up writing a whole story. Listen, if you're talking about boasting, I admit I care the least about that. Yes, I, too, have an ego like anyone else, but I give it little importance. Next, if you talk about encouraging others, I agree—I always encourage people because that way I feel I can win hearts easily and help others achieve great things as well."

"Yes, that way you win hearts. Take me for example. Since that day, I have felt you to be the closest person in my life. In my thirty-two years of life, I have seen nobody like you."

"Since you have expressed so much, let me also share my feelings about you. I feel that someone who can so easily express his heart is one of the simplest people in the world."

"I don't know about that, but I would like to give you some advice: an easy-going person like you always gets hurt in life. This is a suggestion for someone I'm going to pay tribute to in my next book. Therefore, I can only wish her good fortune."

"Oh, but I don't fear getting hurt in life. Pain brings gain, after all. I will keep writing and achieve my goal."

"Amen to that."

"Are you from East Bengal? You behave like one."

"No, I'm a pure West Bengal person with roots here only."

"But I have roots in East Bengal."

"Above all, you are very special to me."

"On that note, we must stop; otherwise, this will keep going all through the night."

"Alright, good night then."

"Okay, good night for today."

After a pause in the conversation, Raktim realized he was not feeling well. A strange sensation ran through his body. Quickly, he opened his shirt collar and sprayed himself with body spray. At the age of thirty-two, for the first time in his life, he began to smell the fragrance of love in his everyday perfume. Raktim laughed at his own condition.

Chapter 9

It is often said that old habits die hard. But then, how does one explain the heavenly occurrence of people falling in love with one another? That is no old habit. Raktim failed to find an answer. What he knew for sure was that relationships change people, and at the end of the day, one naturally gives love and expects love in return. Love can be as much physical as it is emotional. Physical attraction is natural and cannot be denied, even if society maintains a stoic silence on the matter. One can only hope that love and lust are given equal respect and viewed with maturity. Only then can a lover be valued beyond physical desire.

Returning from school, Raktim lost himself while watching the sky absentmindedly. He kept thinking about the relationships in his life that, like the sky above, can be seen but not felt in the flesh. On lonely, cold nights, those connections never brought him any warmth. They existed merely as showpieces in the drawing room of his life.

Since the book fair incident, Raktim had repeatedly logged into Tilottama's Facebook account, liking countless pictures and posting numerous comments, revealing his mad admiration for the girl. He knew such behavior did not suit a thirty-two-year-old mature man like him. But then he remembered the movie *Dil Toh Baccha Hai Ji* (The Heart Is

Always a Child), released in 2011, where Ajay Devgn behaved just as foolishly in love.

That year, in *Dinlipi* magazine, a poem by Tilottama titled *"Earth in Its Silence"* was published. It fascinated Raktim so much that he commented, "I simply fail to express how your poem has touched my heart. You are incredible!"

Tilottama replied, "You keep writing your poetry; only that way will our friendship keep thriving."

Raktim wanted to be honest with himself and with her. So he wrote, "Listen, am I annoying you?"

"Not at all, you have rather amazed me."

"Why is that?"

"Because everything is happening so suddenly since the Book Fair meeting—as if everything is blooming with the redness of the flame-of-the-forest. I wonder if I have suddenly discovered a flower that announces spring in my life!"

"Wow, your words are giving birth to a new poem now!"

"So then, assure me: since you have arrived unannounced in my life, please don't vanish that way."

Raktim knew some requests are meant to be answered only with silence. Such silence is a mark of respect. Above all, nobody knows how time will act upon us and how promises will be kept in the course of life. But whether Tilottama could read his measured silence from the other end remained unknown. In the middle of his doubtful thoughts, however, a phone number arrived from her side with a message: "I don't use Messenger much, so keep my WhatsApp number. I feel people who are closer should exchange WhatsApp messages."

Chapter 10

Arghya called Raktim after a long time. They were childhood buddies, classmates since the third standard at Birbhum District School. They even went to the same private tutors in the higher classes. But since then, they had been busy building their individual careers. After completing his B.Pharm and MBA from Bangalore, Arghya settled in Kolkata and was now living in a rented 2BHK flat in Patuli. He managed the marketing department of a popular pharmaceutical company in the city. His wife, Priyanka, who hailed from Sinthi, was three years younger than he. It reminded Raktim that Tilottama was also three years younger than he.

Arghya wanted to buy a 3BHK property in Rajarhat. He had called to congratulate Raktim because Raktim's newly published four-format board-bound volume of poetry had already gained popularity on social media, and like others, it had caught Arghya's attention too. Like a proud friend, he rang Raktim to wish him more success in life. Arghya also informed him about another childhood friend, Dibyajyoti, who was getting hitched in December. This was news to Raktim, as he had lost touch with Dibyajyoti.

Not only Dibyajyoti, but many of his childhood friends now existed merely as names on Raktim's Facebook friend list. The rat race of life never allowed enough time to go beyond that. While scrolling through the daily dose of the news feed, he saw one friend smiling with his wife in Phuket, another standing in grief before an ICU, a third flashing a victory sign while proudly posing in front of a Royal Enfield showroom with his latest purchase, and possibly a fourth sitting blank-faced on the stairs of a court.

Meanwhile, minutes before hanging up, Arghya asked his friend, "So now, pal, with the new poetry volume in hand, when are you planning to hold the hand of a wife in life?" To this, unknowingly, Raktim replied, "Brother, if a Tilottama comes into my life, even an arid desert will turn into monsoon-drenched Mawsinram."

A perplexed Arghya quipped, "What do you mean by Tilottama? I have never heard of someone by that name!"

Raktim quickly tried to manage the situation and hush everything up with a laugh: "I mean to say that Tilottama Kolkata is calling me, bro."

Chapter 11

"Trust me, dada, I have experience that girls born in May are simply great," Bivash concluded confidently with a puff of his cigarette.

It always amazed Raktim that Bivash, the over-smart twenty-three-year-old that he was, claimed to have so much experience at such a young age. While travelling between the office and home, Raktim sometimes met him. In those short ten minutes, Bivash would smoke at least a couple of cigarettes, say "trust me, dada" half a dozen times, and try to shed light on every serious topic like a celebrated intellectual. However incoherent he might sound, Raktim knew Bivash had a pure heart. And so, he indulged him, saying, "Do you have any more suggestions for me? Let's have another cigarette together!"

"Trust me, dada, we must continue talking with each other. Yes, talking doesn't incur any GST, dollars, or pounds. But there is always a limit to how long one can talk; if your time runs out, you have to give up. In such a situation, you can't even respond to a missed call!"

Raktim finally took his leave, saying, "Well, next time I will keep more time in hand before calling you. Excuse me for now." As he rode away on his bike, Bivash's voice kept echoing behind him, "Trust me, dada...!"

After returning home, Raktim wondered, perhaps foolishly: Could Bivash be right? Why did he say that girls born in May are simply great? Raktim's little research had revealed that Tilottama was born on the fifteenth of May! Did that prove Bivash's claim? *Uff* — he did not want to think about it anymore. Good feelings were filling his mind and heart, uplifting him, and he did not want to spoil them. He was happy. Truly speaking, in those days, his life felt like a new spring, painted in rosy red.

Chapter 12

If someone shares their WhatsApp number in good faith, it does not mean the other person should start pinging them at odd hours. Raktim considered such habits indecent and did not want to be counted among them. So, he decided to continue communicating via Messenger for the next few days. But then, a quick, sharp reply came from Tilottama: "Messenger! Again?"

The way she reacted left Raktim speechless. At that moment, she sent a screenshot of a long list of Messenger messages, many of which had not been opened for days. Some of those, certainly in bad taste, were sent by elderly people. Under the screenshot, Tilottama had written, "Now see and judge for yourself why I avoid opening Messenger mostly. So, I will be happier if you message me on WhatsApp."

Raktim smiled to himself. The girl's way of addressing him was changing with time. He always believed that trust grows gradually and that a distant relationship becomes closer with time. With a content heart, Raktim started writing to Tilottama on WhatsApp with a formal greeting: "*Namaskar!*"

Within a few seconds, the message was seen, but surprisingly, there was no reply. Raktim never expected that. He began writing something, but then deleted everything and put the mobile phone down. A visibly upset Raktim lay down and closed his eyes, hoping to sleep, but his disturbed mind would not let him. The next day, a lump of grey cloud covered his anxious mind, and he understood that the onus for the next move lay on no one but him. He kept searching for a suitable move.

Chapter 13

Areader places a fair amount of importance on a book's cover. So, for his books, Raktim always blindly believed in the talent of Sumanta Adhikari, who was like a brother to him. Sumanta was an Income Tax officer by profession, working in Delhi, but he had a tremendous passion for illustrative artwork. His sketches were the best. Hence, there could have been no one more capable of carefully designing an appropriate cover for *Kheyali Kham*, or *The Envelope of Whims*. Courtesy of that beautiful cover and Raktim's excellent writing, the book left a strong impression on readers.

So, when Raktim discovered that he had missed a call from Sumanta, he quickly called back.

"Hello, brother! Sorry, I missed your call. Please accept my apology."

"It's ok. This is quite natural now since you have become a celebrity."

"Stop! Please don't start all that. Listen—you'll be happy to know that the book and its cover are both very popular. People are appreciating your work."

"I came across your Facebook posts. That's why I'm calling—to congratulate you."

"See, in today's world of thirty-second reels, it's a wonderful thing that people are reading poetry volumes—

lovers are gifting our works to one another. This unimaginable incident is our success!"

"Well, and what about your love life? When are you planning to end your single status?"

"Nope, I'm thinking about marrying someone, probably from Kolkata."

"Wow! Is something cooking up? When you talk like this, I'm sure something has happened."

"Nah! I said it just like that!"

"Okay, I'm hanging up the phone for now. There's a call coming from an unknown number. But I'll definitely call back."

"No problem. Take your time."

After Sumanta's phone call, Raktim paused for a moment and then dialled Tilottama's number. His heart kept pounding as long as the phone kept ringing, until a girl's voice sounded from the other side: "Sorry, yesterday I fell asleep in the middle of the conversation. I could only manage to see your WhatsApp message, but failed to reply."

"Oh, that's okay. Are you doing well?"

"Of course. How are you? By the way, in your DP, I found your girlfriend in your arms. Though I must admit, you two were looking wonderful together."

Chapter 14

Tushar Ray had posted a selfie with Raktim's new poetry volume *Kheyali Kham*, followed by a well-worded review of it. He had even encouraged book lovers to buy and read the book. Since he was tagged in the post, Raktim saw it in his notifications, and it brought a broad smile to his face. After all, Tushar Ray, the man from Birati, was a big name in modern literature. He had a lot of affection for Raktim and constantly kept in touch with him, calling at least once a week and giving him a lot of encouragement for his writing. So, without question, Raktim bowed in respect before such a personality.

Raktim had been writing since his college days and had published his work regularly in magazines and journals whenever he got the chance. His poems were published in the Puja promotions and souvenirs of many Durga Puja and Kali Puja clubs in and around Suri.

Those were his beginning years. Raktim enjoyed seeing his write-ups published from a young age and relished the moments with his parents, Biswanath Babu and Malati Devi. It was during that time that he was introduced to the famous author and poet Tushar Ray through social media. It was from Tushar Ray that Raktim first heard of the concept of invitational writing, in which publishers invite authors to submit their work rather than authors having to approach publishers themselves. Until then, he had always believed that an author had to make the requests. When those requests finally resulted in publications, they gave Raktim a deep sense of satisfaction, and throughout the day, those published works felt like the most precious things in the world.

But now the picture had changed, as requests poured in almost every day, and Raktim often failed to respond to them all. With time, he had become choosy; as his experience grew, he learned that only quality writing should be published so that his readers continued to shower him with love. For a poet like him, quality always mattered. Therefore, he skipped deadlines, ignored calls, even angered some people—yet he shared only those writings he believed would be appreciated by his readers. Publishers, too, eventually came to understand his way of working.

In the College Street area, there was an outlet of *Adya Katha Publication* where Raktim's second poetry volume, *Dak Peon*, was displayed. The owner of the publication, Biman Acharya, sent a text message requesting Raktim to share a poem on the place of religion in the present political scenario and urged him to submit the writing within the next three days, as the *Adya Katha* journal planned to publish its first issue in the third week of the coming month. Raktim replied to the message with a "Certainly!"

Rohit sent a voice message requesting a poem of no more than 20 lines for his magazine *Astha*'s upcoming volume. Raktim repeated his reply, "Certainly!"

Many Lit Fests were being organized, and Raktim routinely received invitations to almost all of them. But due to his job at a school in Suri, it had often proved a daunting task to attend them all. Once, a prominent personality called and invited him to an upcoming Lit Fest. She was poet Keya Sen of

Literature Nowadays. Who could refuse a personality like hers? Shyamali Di and Keya Di were neighbors in an apartment near Subhash Chandra Bose Cancer Hospital, so he was compelled to write, "Certainly!"

Raktim had a strong urge to switch his phone off and forget about it for some time. He was just about to do that when he noticed a 'love-react' to Tushar Ray's praiseworthy post about him. It was none other than Tilottama, and she even added a comment wishing him a bright future.

Chapter 15

While writing—or even studying before writing—Raktim usually kept his phone on silent. But unfortunately that day, he forgot to do that and when it suddenly rang, he got really annoyed. When he glanced at the screen, it showed "Trust Me calling!" It kept ringing, but he did not pick up. When it started ringing again for the second time, however, he was forced to answer.

"Yes, tell me."

"Trust me, dada, this evening I suddenly bumped into my ex-girlfriend Shalini in Dubrajpur! She took out her phone and showed me some pictures taken in Manali with her husband. She asked me how I felt about those! Frankly, her question caught me off guard, and I sheepishly replied, 'Both of you are looking good together,' and then paused before adding, 'like siblings.' However, the treatment I got after that shouldn't be told to anyone!"

Hearing that, Raktim laughed and asked, "Which side of your cheek got reddened for this, by the way? Whatever! Listen, I'm studying now for my next writing. So I should end the call. We will catch up tomorrow."

Raktim again focused on his studies, knowing that a good write-up can only be written with careful research and learning. Writing without background study is sheer foolishness. To produce a good literary work, one has to study decades of masterpieces published by renowned poets and authors. People who fall into the rat race of writing run behind recognition and felicitation programs, forgetting the very purpose of entering the world of literature, the very worship of art and words.

Raktim had heard that one has to lobby hard to survive in Bengal's literary market and get regularly invited to events for recognition and publicity. Not only that, to win praise, limelight, and validation, many groups grow like banana groves on social media. Thousands join just to earn quick fame. These groups are filled with sheer madness, where countless low-quality posts are shared, and good works are easily buried under the trash. Naturally, Raktim long ago lost interest in such groups. Apart from them, elderly groups have also formed locally under the name of literary societies across the districts of Bengal, where over-enthusiasts make a beeline not to discuss literature, but to indulge in slander and gossip. Both sides surely lack the responsibility and commitment needed to contribute something valuable to society through their writings. Good authors are never impressed by them, nor do these people show any respect for good authors. Instead, such parasites attract young people seeking quick fame, leading them astray. They organize memorials for deceased members, loudly lamenting great losses without considering who else in the world actually cares. Soon, they run out of enthusiasm and shut down their activities.

Truly speaking, Raktim had seen such groups up close. He now laughed at them. He never even dreamt of publishing a whole book in his name—he only wished to stay immersed in reading, writing, and crafting quality literary works. His resolve, perseverance, and commitment finally bore fruit, making his dream come true. Just as a river flows past civilization after civilization along its course, a human life, too, flows through relationships and bonds of love and affection.

Raktim's thoughts reminded him of Tilottama's words, and he felt a deep burn in his heart. How can people be so judgmental in sensitive matters without even reading the captions on uploaded photographs? It's ridiculous! Raktim had made the girl Ayantika his sister; she was twelve years younger than he. They had met at a music programme in Suri three years ago. Since then, they had never missed Rakhi or Bhaiphonta. It's true that for the rest of the year, the girl hardly appears around Raktim, but she always makes a point of being present on those two occasions. Yet Tilottama completely misunderstood seeing her beside him, so much so that Raktim had to take a lot of pain to clarify the situation. Thankfully, in the end, Tilottama concluded the call on a good note, saying "Take care and tata" in a deep voice.

Chapter 16

"So, what's your next plan in life?" Lisa asked after taking a long sip from her coffee mug.

"First, come clear on what you mean when you say planning!" Raktim chuckled.

"Well, I mean that you should select a suitable partner to marry and settle down with. After all, you are financially stable with a government job in hand. Your parents are old enough and must be expecting such mature steps from you."

"Maybe you're right, but I need some more time."

"And may I ask why?"

Raktim sipped his coffee slowly while answering, "I have noticed friends all around suffering from premature marriage failures — many of which perhaps lasted only a few months since I attended their wedding receptions."

Lisa finished her coffee and looked seriously at Raktim. "See, accidents happen when one starts driving on the streets, but that doesn't mean everyone will stop driving."

Raktim smiled. "To tell you the truth, I have fallen in love with a girl from Kolkata. We regularly talk over the phone, though I have never invited her on a cozy date."

Lisa paused a bit and then said, "See, taking your book *Envelope of Whims* in my hand, I urge you to figure out your intention in marrying her. Make it fast, because I know how whimsical you are!"

After paying the coffee bill, both came out of the restaurant. Raktim went closer to Lisa and informed her in a low voice, "This twelfth of April, we are meeting in Kolkata — she called me."

"Now that's awesome news. Have a blast, dear!"

"Thanks."

After seeing off Lisa, Raktim took out his phone to call Raqib.

"Yes, *bhaijan*! All is well?"

"Yes, all's well. Listen, come the day after tomorrow, around ten in the morning, with your car. I will go to Kolkata."

"Sure, brother. I will arrive on time. I mean, I have no problem. Which day of the week is it?"

"It's a Tuesday. Make sure you wake up early and come on time."

Raktim hung up and started walking toward his home. He could not deny the fact that during those days, he did not take much interest in life around him because he kept waiting all day for the night, when, after dinner, he could retire quickly to his bed and wait for Tilottama's phone call. He made sure the phone stayed fully charged and remained undisturbed — available only to her. Raktim questioned his own craziness many a time, wondering how, at such a mature age, one could become so stupid and hopelessly romantic. Every time, Rabindranath Tagore's *Jiban Smriti* smiled back with silent replies!

Chapter 17

Book fairs have an indigenous scent. From district book fairs to the Kolkata Book Fair, everywhere, Raktim felt that the smell hardly changed. It was the twelfth of April, and a book fair–cum–lit fest had been going on at College Square since the eighth of April. Raktim and Tilottama had decided to meet and spend some intimate time together.

The car carrying Raktim flew over the Maa Flyover as fast as it could, but it still took some time to reach Garia. There was a coffee shop called *Canava* there, where Tilottama planned to meet him around three in the afternoon. Raktim had set the shop's GPS location on Raqib's mobile. Such technology has undoubtedly made life easier these days, but Raktim always knew that not all distances in life can be bridged through technology. He threw his cigarette butt out of the car window and felt a sense of restlessness, driven by a strong urge to see Tilottama.

"Do not call or even text me during my work. I will reach the place at three, taking a half-day leave from the office. Have faith. Bye for now."

'Faith' is a word probably lost in oblivion since the death of Adam Faith and his now-forgotten '60s chartbuster: *What do you want if you don't want money? What do you want if you don't want gold? Say what you want, and I'll give it to you, darling! Wish you wanted my love, baby!*

After the spell of thinking ended, Raktim quipped, "Raqib, hope you're not facing a problem driving with the GPS guidance?"

"No, brother. We will arrive at the location soon."

"Okay."

In the last few years, as Raktim had begun practicing serious writing in the literary world, he had noticed that people from Kolkata have a curious, often amusing fascination with Shantiniketan. As a result, numerous stay options, such as bungalows and homestays, have sprung up around the Shantiniketan Sonajhuri Haat. Many from Kolkata have either bought or booked those places to spend leisure time there before returning to the hustle and bustle of city life. Raktim agreed that one should respect the love for a place, but not the exaggerated show-offs. Yesterday, he went for a bike ride to Shantiniketan because, at the *Boiwala Book Café*, one can get tastefully designed coffee cups and T-shirts as gifts. He picked a beautiful red cup for Tilottama with *And Shantiniketan* scribbled on it. He had also bought a large box of dark chocolates, which was now on the way.

Seconds were turning into hours, and his heart was pounding fast. Raktim quickly checked his watch and found it was already a quarter past three. He had parked his car just in front of the café while waiting. Now he spotted a small tea shop at a corner, with an empty bench inviting people like him. Since texting and calling were forbidden at that moment, and having faith was the only option, he felt handicapped and helpless.

"Raqib, go and ask for two cups of tea from the shop. I'll be behind you."

Raqib followed orders and asked for two cups of black tea without sugar. The woman running the shop did not even look up and promptly prepared the tea. Raktim lit his second cigarette to suppress his anxiety and stepped forward for the tea. The song playing in the shop was *For auld lang syne, my jo, for auld lang syne, we'll take a cup of kindness yet, for auld lang syne.* By the time he finished his tea and was sinking into a sense of dejection, his phone rang. He picked up immediately, and there was Tilottama's voice on the other side: "Where are you?"

"A furlong away from the café you asked me to be at. In a tea shop."

"Well, I'm standing at the café entrance."

"Okay, I'm coming."

"Hmm, come quickly."

Raktim could clearly see her after just a quick step forward. And he felt that he was born to be there. She was wearing grey sunglasses, a side bag hanging from her shoulder, and holding an umbrella. Raktim was too impressed but did not express it. Instead, he said, "I've checked some wonderful reviews about this café on Google."

Tilottama replied, "But this café is very pricey. We can go to the Coffee House instead, if you like."

"Coffee House! Wow!" Raktim was pleasantly surprised and immediately opened the back seat door for Tilottama. He took the front seat next to Raqib because he felt the lady might be uncomfortable sitting beside an unknown person in the back seat during their very first meeting. This time, he did not care about his ironed shirt getting creased by the front seat belt.

Chapter 18

Raktim once fell in love with Sudipa Roy in 2012. He took the girl to a sweetshop in Suri one evening to propose. At a young age, he thought that having sweets while ushering in a new beginning for a fresh relationship was a noble idea. But when she gulped around four *rosogollas*, one after another, Raktim wasted no more time and quickly proposed to her. However, Sudipa's reaction was very poised. She took her time finishing the sweets first with water and then replied, "See, Raktim, in this matter we are similar. I too like girls!" That night, Raktim could not even have his dinner properly. Later, he understood that he had only a passing infatuation with Sudipa.

Raktim silently pinched himself to confirm that he was not dreaming. Tilottama was sitting in the back seat of the car, for real, watching the fast-moving scenes of busy city life through the car window. She had removed her sunglasses, keeping the bag and the umbrella by her side. It would still take some more time to reach Coffee House, making their way through the busy roads of Garia. The weather, meanwhile, had changed from bright and sunny to dreamy and greyish. A romantic audio series started playing on the car radio. Looking at the empty balconies of the city's high-rises and the jostling crowds on the pavements, Raktim realized that people rush only to return to the arms of their loved ones. Without your loved ones, there is no meaning in life.

The silence in the car soon felt odd to Raktim, and he wished to break it. So he asked Tilottama, "All well at home?"

"Yes. What about you?"

"Same. All good."

"And how is your favorite Ayantika?"

Tilottama's question took all the air out of Raktim, and he timidly answered, "We have actually not been in touch for many days. However, I know that she is studying music in a girls' college in Bolpur. But listen—after reaching College Street, we will first search for a convenient place to park the car and then enter the Coffee House."

"Sure. And this is for you." Tilottama extended a book to him.

Raktim took the book in hand and found it was a poetry book with a yellow jacket cover that read, *Romance and Poems of Hibernation*.

"There is a poem of mine in it. Please read and give your views."

Raktim turned the pages and found Poet Tilottama Mukhopadhyay's name among the top entries in the contents list. He nodded and whispered that Tilottama was the best, but aloud he said, "Sure, I will read and let you know what I feel. That's a promise."

As soon as they reached the entrance to the Coffee House, a visibly excited Tilottama announced, "Wow, we're standing before a building visited by hundreds of renowned personalities. The famous Coffee House!"

Raktim followed Tilottama while climbing upstairs. They found that only the front table was empty, and the rest were occupied. Patrons were crowding every table, both there and downstairs. There was a banner advertising a Holiday Home at Digha on the far wall. Sitting down, both felt short of words as they looked deeply into each other's eyes. But then Raktim took the lead in breaking the silence. "Though I can't say that I'm disliking the place, still, may I ask why we didn't try sitting downstairs somewhere?"

Tilottama smiled radiantly at his question. "Downstairs is for seniors, and upstairs is for lovebirds. It's a thumb rule."

Raktim almost melted at such a candid confession. To avoid more such words, he hastily tried to change the topic. "I found a small book-selling outlet at the entry gate. Isn't it a good idea to keep a few copies of my book *Envelope of Whims* there?"

"Hmm," Tilottama replied monosyllabically.

"So, what should we have here?" Raktim again tried to change the subject quickly.

"We shouldn't miss the coffee here, what do you say?" She looked at him with appealing eyes.

"Sure," Raktim tried to bury his excitement by adding a hint of smartness to his voice.

"Well, then order the coffee for us," Tilottama answered calmly.

"Okay, but someone has to come to take the order at least. Can you see anyone around? None. Isn't it ridiculous?" Raktim's nerves caught up with him, and he started feeling irritated at the difficulty of hiding his nervousness.

But Tilottama nodded with a smile. "Here, couples are generally allowed some space to get comfortable with each other first. Then, when they get engaged in a cosy conversation, the bearer arrives to take the order. Old custom!"

Proving her right, a bearer appeared at their table. Raktim promptly ordered two cups of hot coffee. After the man left, Raktim brought out the pack of dark chocolate and gifted it to Tilottama. She accepted it with a broad grin and added, "I also brought some chocolate for you, but forgot to give it to you in the car." She then carefully put her new gift in her side bag and took out a box of chocolates, a pen, and a magazine. "A teacher should always be gifted a pen," she said.

Her words made him emotional. He found them fascinating and spellbinding. He slowly set the chocolate box aside on the table and opened the magazine. He was pleasantly surprised to find Tilottama's name at the beginning of the contents page. He did not hide his feelings and, in one breath, he went on and on, "Wow! Awesome! *Avidipta* or 'Great Illumination' is one of the top-level magazines around. So, it feels great to find your poetry at the start of such a prestigious publication. Now, can you sign your name at the top of your poem for me with your newly gifted pen?"

The coffee arrived at the table, along with his request. Tilottama sipped the coffee and lovingly obliged. She signed 'Tilottama Mukhopadhyay' beside the title of her poem, *Post Box,* in the magazine.

Tilottama had completed her postgraduate studies in Bengali and was working at a private firm near Garia. Therefore, she had to commute daily by train from Madhyamgram to Garia. Being the only child, she was dearly loved by her parents. She went on with her stories, a loving smile at the corner of her lips, to the eager ears of Raktim, who kept praying that time stop ticking and she continue, at least for the next three hundred years. Raktim clearly understood that he was head over heels in love with the girl.

"If you don't mind, can I hold your hand, please?" Raktim asked.

Tilottama offered her hand without any questions. He held it. And at that very moment, a man arrived with their coffee bill at the table. Unperturbed, Raktim immediately ordered two more coffees and sent him away, determined to extend this beautiful moment.

Chapter 19

A few months earlier, Raktim had read on social media that good girls are no longer seen in reality, but only in books and films. He could feel how false those words were.

"Tilottama! Can you do me a favor? Never leave me, please. I will be ruined otherwise, and I'm not exaggerating my feelings."

"But, Sir, we must leave. It's necessary now; otherwise, we can't reach the College Square Book Fair."

Her words broke his trance. Coming back to reality, Raktim quickly paid the bills, gave some tips too, and left the Coffee House. They took some memorable selfies on the way, and Raktim lovingly put Tilottama's gifts into his red bag.

While they were having a good time at the Coffee House, Raktim noticed couples scribbling their names on the walls, pledging to stay together for eternity. It is not important whether those names will stay together forever after the pledge, but what is important is those beautiful moments of togetherness, which will, of course, stay memorable. Then, one day, a fresh coat of paint will wipe those names from the walls, thus making space for new sets of lovers to write their names again.

Raktim kept walking with Tilottama through the Book Fair ground, thinking about these things, when Tilottama suddenly broke his thoughts. "Will you have phuchka? Like curd-phuchka? Don't worry, I will pay."

Raktim asked, "It hardly matters who is paying, but the question is, should we have curd-phuchka after coffee with milk? Isn't that an absurd idea?"

Ignoring Raktim's doubt, Tilottama stood in line at the phuchka counter. While having curd-phuchka, they clicked selfies again, making golden memories, oblivious to the hustle and bustle of College Street and grateful to life for the good moments it gives. But amidst beautiful things, misfortune often occurs. So it did there, when over a trivial matter, a rickshaw-puller and a beggar started quarrelling, hurling abuses at each other. The phuchka seller tried to interfere, but in vain. Within moments, the situation became uncomfortable, and they tried their best to finish the food quickly. Tilottama paid the money as fast as she could. Raktim took her by his side and took long strides in search of better peace — perhaps adorned with books they thought of writing together, possibly laced with Rabindra Sangeet.

Walking hand in hand through the busy College Street, Raktim suddenly noticed Tilottama laughing to herself. He understood that the whole incident of their fleeing from the wrangle was making her laugh. Raktim enjoyed every moment as her laughter spread like a string of pearls, like a gush of spring, and he kept drenching underneath.

Chapter 20

Tilottama stopped a while in front of the Book Fair entrance and quickly took a picture of the gate. Then, moving ahead, they found a poetry session underway, with poets crowding the stage and a handful of elderly people seated in blue plastic chairs. Nearby, enthusiastic parents were preparing their children, probably for the upcoming dance program. Tilottama clicked a photo of them from a distance. As Raktim kept looking at her, she turned around and said, "Let's not visit any stall today. Rather, why don't we find some space for us, where there will be none but the two of us!" Raktim could hardly want anything more than that. He wondered how she could speak what he could not. With a little effort, they found a deserted spot between two stalls, where a dim piece of darkness had tiptoed in stealthily.

In front of them, the water of the College Square pool was dancing in the glitters of the colored glow of the fairy lights, with Rabindra Sangeet as its worthy accompaniment, telling people around that, with love and gentle care, my friend, do etch my name in the secluded shrine of your heart. Raktim felt amazed by the sight of Tilottama standing still, perhaps in a trance, lost in thought, gazing into the darkness. Raktim lit a cigarette silently and waited, looking ahead at the shimmering water in the dark background. He felt that he would always remain indebted to moments like this.

"Have some lemon tea. Will you?"

A tea-seller called from behind, breaking the effervescent silence.

"Yes, give us two," Raktim stubbed the cigarette under his feet and turned to the man.

They had their tea in silence, and Raktim felt that time was infinite, endless, and immortal. He witnessed how, in the evening breeze, Tilottama's hair flew, partially covering her face, and from that partially covered face, she looked like the idol of a Goddess. Immersed in his thoughts, Raktim lightly touched her hair and moved it aside to have a closer look at the idol's face. Then Tilottama buried her face in Raktim's chest and suddenly asked, in a very low voice, "Will you still love me the same when I get married to my fiancé Samarpan?"

Chapter 21

During their school days in Birbhum, Arghya and Raktim used to exchange *Asterix* comics and discuss the wonderful adventures of Asterix and Obelix. They learnt that Obelix did not fear anything in the world except that the sky might fall on the earth one day. His fear used to be the funniest thing to them in their childhood because they thought it was impossible. But, at this age, Raktim understood what it meant to have the sky fall on his head when he discovered one Samarpan as the third point of the triangle, standing far away like a gloomy nemesis. By that time, Tilottama had started narrating, "I have been in love with Samarpan since our university days. He lives in Sonarpur and works in the corporate sector at an office in New Town. Our families have already given their consent to our relationship. But since I never discuss my private life in public, I have always kept my relationship status on social media as 'single'. All was going well until I met you that day at the Book Fair. Believe me, since you came into my life, I feel completely lost."

By the time Raktim lit another cigarette, he could feel tears rolling down his cheek. He could barely whisper, holding on to the last straw of hope deep inside himself, and asked Tilottama, "So, now what have you decided?"

Tilottama replied while weeping, "We have finalized our marriage date on the twenty-second of December this year."

Raktim remembered that in school they had studied that the twenty-second of December marks the shortest day and the longest night of the year. Evidently, that day would indeed usher in the longest night in Raktim's life. Raktim silently stubbed out the burnt cigarette and lit another because he felt that only nicotine could stimulate some energy inside him. But Tilottama held his hand tightly and pleaded, "Raktim, please don't act like this. Try to understand my situation. There is no lie in my love for you. So please don't hurt yourself."

Raktim was struggling to reply, but he did not get a chance, as Tilottama's phone suddenly started ringing. Raktim could see that the call was coming from Samarpan. Tilottama quickly moved away and took the call. She finished her conversation over the phone and came back to Raktim to say, "Listen, Raktim, what do you think? Have we made any mistakes by loving each other?"

Raktim paused for a moment and then answered, "In the middle of a world full of politics of hate and religion, where one mostly finds people killing each other, when people like us fall in love with each other, certainly, there's nothing wrong in that. We made no mistake."

Chapter 22

Meanwhile, at the book fair, the Rabindra Sangeet stopped playing because it was almost time to close for the day. But the two of them never cared about how long they had been standing there on the grounds or what was happening around them. At last, Raktim said, "Okay, let's move. I need to go."

Tilottama replied in a low voice, "Can we stay a little longer?"

The man selling lemon tea approached them again, but this time they ignored him. Raktim looked at his watch and told her again, "We have to leave now."

Tilottama pleaded once more, "No. Please stay a little more."

Raktim said nothing. He felt that even the flow of time sometimes chooses to stop on its own. But when, after a while, Tilottama still refused to move, Raktim held her hands and said, "Look! I will give you a lift in my car to Madhyamgram. We're running late, so you won't have to travel alone. Please keep in mind that, at this late hour of the night, your safety and security are now my responsibility."

He held her by the hand and slowly guided her to the car park outside the College Square Book Fair grounds. He paid the parking fee and asked Raqib, "Did you get something to eat?"

"*Bhaijan*, yes—though I didn't have any junk food."

"Okay, then let's first travel up to Madhyamgram. I'm fixing the location on your mobile. On the way, we will have biriyani somewhere."

"Alright, *bhaijan*."

Now Raktim sat beside Tilottama in the back seat, on her left.

"Let me set my home location in my office phone. You follow the location and accordingly drop me," she said.

Raqib took the phone from her. Meanwhile, a dejected and visibly perplexed Raktim, overwhelmed by the chain of events, fished out the coffee mug he had bought for Tilottama and handed it to her.

"I bought this for you. Sorry that I forgot to give it to you earlier."

"This is simply awesome! And how wonderfully it has *And Shantiniketan* written on it!"

Raktim remained silent. Their car was speeding past the city at night, and he watched it through the window. Then he turned towards Tilottama, silently took her hand, closed his eyes, and leaned back in his seat. Until now, he had never touched a woman like this, nor had he ever felt the warmth of a woman's body. A mild trace of excitement stirred deep within him. He kept his eyes closed, secretly wishing to prolong the moment. But soon, Tilottama gently pulled her hand away from his. Instead, she touched his forehead and hesitantly asked, "Hey, Raktim, are you running a fever? I think you have a high temperature."

Raktim felt embarrassed and replied quickly, "Uh, no, I'm fine." Then he immediately turned to Raqib and ordered, "Hey Raqib! We'll stop at that restaurant ahead."

They had chicken biriyani together at the restaurant and clicked some photographs. By the time they started again for Madhyamgram, they were already running late. Tilottama received a call from her mother, asking why she was delayed, especially when she traveled the same route every day after office.

Once the car reached a busy crossing in Madhyamgram, it was time for Tilottama to say goodbye.

"See you. Please text me after you reach Suri. Get some sleep in the car."

She waved, got out of the vehicle with her belongings, and walked away smiling.

After she left, Raktim felt an infinite emptiness on his right side in the back seat. Raqib turned the car around and suddenly shouted, "*Bhaijan*! It seems Madam has left her office phone in the car!"

Raktim cried, "Oh, no!" and quickly leapt out of the car, running in the direction Tilottama had gone only minutes earlier, holding her phone. It was an awkward journey for him—he did not know the roads, and the people around looked at him strangely, as though he were an outsider. At last, he spotted Tilottama walking about fifty meters ahead. Breathlessly, he managed to shout, "Tilottama... your phone... your phone!" Then he stopped, panting heavily.

Tilottama heard him and rushed back. She opened her water bottle and made him drink. Then she said, distressed, "I'm so sorry. Because of my forgetfulness, you had to take so much trouble. I made you run along an unknown road at this hour. I feel so guilty."

Raktim looked deeply into her eyes and said clearly, "Tilottama, I can even travel a light-year for you, if required."

Chapter 23

Joyee Ganguly, originally from Rampurhat, was in her first year of Mass Communication and Journalism at Vidyasagar College in Suri. She stayed as a paying guest with another girl, near the college, at an elderly lady's house. Once, a neighborhood uncle insisted that Raktim visit a local theater group called *Abohoman — The Unceasing* — for a few days, much against his will. Initially, he tried to reason with him, saying that although he was into writing, he could never actually act. However, it was at the theater group that Raktim met Joyee.

Earlier that evening, Raktim and Raqib had their dinner at a roadside food joint called Nabanna. After dinner, Raktim lazily lit a cigarette and kept staring blankly at the winding, vast highway lying there like a dark, long snake, where scores of cars sped through the darkness, tearing the silence of the night. He kept remembering the incidents that had taken place throughout the day. Restlessly, he brushed through his long, dark, unkempt hair. And just at that very moment, his phone rang. Joyee was calling! It surprised him that she called at such a late hour. Raktim took his time to pick up.

"Hello!"

"Brother, did I disturb your sleep? Did I disturb you?"

"Not at all. I'm travelling back from Kolkata to Suri."

"Okay, fine. Listen, I made a blunder today, and I badly need some help from you."

"What happened?"

"This evening I rode with my boyfriend, David, to the fast-food corner at the Suri bus stand to have an egg roll and, unfortunately, got caught by my landlady. She scolded me a lot before allowing me back into the house."

Raktim expressed surprise, "Well, I don't understand here how I can help you?"

Joyee said, "Brother, under her intense questioning, I became nervous and gave your WhatsApp number as the contact for my local guardian!"

Raktim screamed, "What! What will I do if she calls me?"

"Please, brother, if she calls, somehow manage her. David and I are madly in love. I know only you can handle a situation like this. Please!"

"Hmm, those who can't fulfil their own dreams can go to any extent to help fulfil others'. Don't get tense. I will see to it."

"What do you mean by that?"

"Nothing. Good night," Raktim cut the call quickly and boarded the car. He asked Raqib, "Name your favorite Bollywood movie."

Raqib was chewing tobacco. He paused and replied, "*Devdas*. The one with Shah Rukh Khan."

Chapter 24

Usually, when Bivash called, Raktim could only manage to utter, "Tell me," because after that, Bivash never gave him a chance to speak, continuously blabbering—mostly about his latest life experiences. Take, for example, the incident when Bivash called, he immediately started, "Trust me, brother, a beautiful girl called Sagarika Sen sent me a friend request a few months back. Like young men of my age, I accepted the request. Then we kept giving love reactions to each other's pictures and posting praise-filled comments. One night, the beauty even stepped into my dreams from the wall of my Facebook account. The next day, I found that the girl had changed her Facebook DP to her mother's picture. The lady looked to be at least fifty-five years old. I gave a love reaction to the picture and posted a comment: 'Take my *pranam*, aunty.' A few minutes later, my beautiful lady wrote me, for the first time, a long message in Messenger: 'Listen, have you gone nuts? After posting my daughter's pictures for so long, I finally made up my mind to post my own picture as the DP — and you made such a crazy comment! Ridiculous!'"

Raktim kept his reply short: "Then?"

Bivash replied, "Trust me, bro, sometimes when I revisit my block list, it reminds me of these types of incidents! I wish to tell you about another such incident involving a girl. Her name was... umm... Oh, I think I forgot her name!"

"Fine, remember her name first, and then call me back," Raktim said, disconnecting the phone, and then mindlessly opened his Facebook.

It was thanks to Facebook that Raktim had been connected with Suvrajit from Dumdum and Soumyadip from Chandannagar since he was just eighteen. While Suvrajit worked in the Excise Department, Soumyadip was still searching for a good job. Though they often planned a meetup, they still could not fix a date. Finally, they had a good time together with Raktim, and now they were all on a drive. It was the fifteenth of May, 2015. They went for a cruise on the Ganges and enjoyed a Hindi musical programme on board. It was raining lightly, and they happily got wet. Suvrajit took photographs with his newly bought DSLR camera.

After the cruise, during their drive, Raktim asked Suvrajit, "Do you have any idea why Kolkata is called the City of Joy?" Suvrajit replied, "See, in Kolkata, there are people whose income crosses one crore and people who hardly manage to earn even a hundred rupees every day, but the fun fact is that both of them live happily here in their sweet little ways."

Raktim felt that he had truly fallen in love with Kolkata in his own way and said, "Wow! That's really nice to learn."

All this while Soumyadip did not speak, but suddenly he asked Raqib, "Brother, please let us get down at the next turning, before the Enfield showroom. We are to meet another friend here after a long time."

They waved back at Raktim, smiling, after getting out of the car. Raktim asked Raqib to head straight to Jadavpur.

Raktim had probably been waiting for this day. It was Tilottama's birthday. Yesterday, at midnight, he had sent her a birthday wish over WhatsApp. He made no calls, though, because Tilottama told him that, on her birthday every year, she and Samarpan had long phone conversations. Also, Raktim noticed on Truecaller that Tilottama had been "On a call" for a long time. He consoled himself with the words that even time needed time to settle down. But still, a restless mind disturbed his sleep.

He kept squirming in bed all night, smoked cigarette after cigarette, tried in vain to calm himself down, and struggled to stop his tears, thinking about the well-being of Tilottama. Being a true lover, he felt that he should never tarnish her beautiful future with his tears. He knew both of them were truthful to each other and genuinely loved each other—because love knows no reason. But then, Tilottama never hid her commitment to Samarpan either, whereas Raktim had actually gone much deeper into his feelings without asking Tilottama or knowing about Samarpan. At such a ripe age, it is never easy to back out of love, and therefore, Raktim naturally felt depressed.

He had reserved a room at a hotel called *Cacophony Inn* in Jadavpur well in advance. It was where he was staying now with Raqib. It was a good hotel, though, including the parking charges, it turned out to be a bit expensive. There was a restaurant on the ground floor, and one could easily order food from there. Raktim found that Raqib had fallen asleep, so he slowly made his way to the hotel balcony. The whole day, he had never tried to call her. But now, when he rang her number, what did he hear? He heard a female voice announcing, "The number you have dialled is out of reach of a failed lover like you."

Before closing his eyes, he could make out that the pavement underneath was not far down from the balcony.

Chapter 25

One cannot deny that there is a dark side to the Bengali literary world, and anyone who works in this world for a considerable period will agree. A number of men who earn some recognition after writing books for quite some time turn into predators and start harassing young women, fans and writers alike. They hunt them down by luring them with achievements and accolades. Tilottama too had been a victim of this system a few years back, when an established Bengali writer, Sanjiv Karmakar, almost got hold of her with his shrewd and vicious motives. She tactfully freed herself and maintained a safe distance. This was followed by her losing invitations to write for quite a few renowned magazines, for reasons unknown. Not only that, but her published writings were also removed overnight from some journals without her being informed.

Tilottama tried to hold herself together during such a tough time and kept herself busy with studies and other work, repeating to herself that such nuisances were only a part of life. She never complained to anyone, but with Raktim's recommendation, she recently published some of her work in good journals, which were well received by readers. Raktim took pride in her growing fame. He could not stay away for a day without thinking about her.

With mounting disappointment and anxiety, coupled with sleeplessness, Raktim suddenly fell from the hotel balcony, suffering a nervous breakdown that day. His mobile phone fell away from him. It was only when Raqib arrived at the balcony for a quick smoke that he discovered Raktim and somehow managed to carry him back to the room and splash water on him to revive him. The hotel authorities then brought in a local doctor, and Raktim received proper medical treatment. He felt better after some time, but could not speak with Tilottama that day. After recovering, when he finally took his mobile phone from Raqib, he found the display completely cracked—just like his mind.

Chapter 26

Raktim had been wearing glasses since his school days, when he was in class seven. The doctor had strictly instructed him never to remove them except while bathing or sleeping. At first, following the doctor's instructions troubled him a lot, but gradually it became a habit. However, during the COVID period, the trouble returned when the mask covered his face, causing his glasses to fog up. Tilottama had expressed significant dissatisfaction with Raktim's glass frame in the past.

Raktim never told his parents about his health issues during his visit to Kolkata on the occasion of Tilottama's birthday because he did not want to make them anxious. He called his school from Raqib's phone and informed them that, due to an exigency, he would be taking a few more days of casual leave. In between, Raktim got a new display protector for his broken phone from a shop near his hotel. The shopkeeper was peculiar because, for reasons unknown, the lad looked into his eyes and, in a deep voice, said, "Do come whenever you need anything, because from phone set to heart, I can heal everything."

Raktim answered sternly while paying, "Sorry! I don't walk your path."

On Monday after office, Raktim met Tilottama, gifted her a large pack of dark chocolates, and wished her a belated birthday. But Tilottama protested his use of the word *'belated'* and said she never thought he was late, since he had already wished her on WhatsApp at midnight. Then she added, "And I knew you would surely come today, and that's why I brought these things for you."

She extended a pair of new glasses and a wallet. Raktim was pleasantly surprised. "Wow! But why are you gifting me when it is your birthday?"

Tilottama smiled lightly. "Do change your glasses when you go back home. Moreover, at our first meeting at the Book Fair, I noticed that your wallet also requires an immediate change."

Raktim felt stumped at her words.

Finding him silent, Tilottama went on, "While coming to the office, I forgot to bring my lunch box in a rush. At the office, due to work pressure, I couldn't have anything more than tea. So now that we have some time on our hands, let's go get some food together."

Raktim proposed, "While coming, I saw a KFC outlet. Should we go there?"

After a quick thought, she agreed. "Okay, let's go."

After a short ride, they could see the KFC joint. Tilottama chose to stay in the car, so Raktim bought combo parcels for them. He sat in the back seat on her right, extended a food pack to Raqib, and said, "Have it after we return to the hotel."

Hearing that, Tilottama asked, "Will you not return to Suri today?"

Raktim replied briefly, "No," and added, "Due to some reasons, I took a couple of days' leave from work; hence, I'll be in Kolkata."

Now Raqib asked, "I mean, then should I drive towards Madhyamgram?" Both were surprised at his words, and then both laughed out loud. When the car started, it drove mindlessly for some time along the Kolkata city bypass. Raqib turned on some light music on the car's FM channel. All felt the romance of the night in the metro city. Tilottama and Raktim started feeding each other lovingly by the time the car ascended the Maa Flyover. Slowly, they passed the huge structures of the five-star luxury hotels ITC Sonar Bangla, ITC Royal Bengal, and JW Marriott. The magic of the Kolkata night usurped their minds and souls.

Tilottama asked absent-mindedly, "Why are we roaming like two careless, free-spirited souls? Why is everything looking so beautiful around?"

Raktim joked with Raqib, "Can you drive your brother and sister-in-law straight to Suri now?"

Raqib and Tilottama both laughed. Raktim felt his untold misery vanish in seconds like camphor before this roll of laughter.

In less than half an hour, they reached Madhyamgram, and the stretch through which they were passing was mostly deserted and dark for want of street lights, with shady trees on both sides. Raqib suddenly stopped the car by the roadside. The engine's silence quickly soaked into the quintessential stillness of the atmosphere.

"What happened? Why did you stop?" Raktim quipped.

Raqib quickly replied, "There is a lovely biriyani shop in sight. Aren't you getting the smell of food? I'll rush to get some for you two."

Finishing his words, Raqib jumped out of the car and sprinted to the biriyani shop. And in that beautiful opportunity, Tilottama grabbed the collars of Raktim's shirt with both hands and pressed her lips to his, as firmly as she could.

Chapter 27

There is a Latin phrase, *carpe diem,* which means to make the most of the present and give little thought to the future. Raktim also believed in living life to the fullest, as long as he had the chance to live alongside Tilottama.

Raktim woke up and switched off the ringing alarm. Then he opened Google to check the location of Priya Cinema Hall and the distance between Garia and Rashbehari Avenue. Next, he went to the bathroom to freshen up and get ready for the day. When the doorbell rang, he opened it and was pleasantly surprised to find Raqib, all ready and chewing paan. As soon as Raktim said, "We will be leaving by ten, so quickly take out the car," Raqib merely shrugged and replied, "Sure, brother!" Without losing any more time, both of them went downstairs to the ground floor of the hotel. Just outside the hotel, there were a handful of small shops selling hot tea, biscuits, and cigarettes. From one such shop, they finished their breakfast.

The private firm where Tilottama worked had a strict rule that deducted salary even for one day of absence. Very late last night, Tilottama sent Raktim a voice message, informing him that she had tried very hard and had finally managed to secure two days' leave from her office, and that during those two days, she would be by his side. Raktim typed his surprise: "But that means a deduction of two days' salary for you!" To this she replied, "Let that be! I have lost a lot in life already."

Then she sent another message: "Tomorrow, please pick me up from Garia Crossing. I bought two movie tickets for us. Corner seats!"

It was still ten minutes to ten when Raqib and Raktim parked the car slightly ahead of Garia Crossing and began to wait. It is true that waiting is another name for time! Raktim's eyes wandered to a butcher's shop. Surprisingly, there was a flower shop right beside it. He went to that shop and bought some red roses for Tilottama, placing them back inside the car. As his watch struck ten, he reached for his phone—but then he saw Tilottama walking toward him with a radiant smile on her lips.

As Raktim was handing Tilottama the bunch of roses, Raqib made the moment memorable by switching on the car's FM radio, where Raktim's favourite KK was singing one of his chartbuster romantic numbers. Tilottama bent towards him to take the roses and lovingly fondled the tuft of hair falling over his forehead. It felt heavenly to Raktim.

Chapter 28

It was not the COVID era, but some people were still wearing masks. Tilottama did the same when entering the Priya cinema hall. In her case, however, Raktim knew the real reason she hid her face behind the mask. While coming, Raktim had handed Raqib three hundred rupees and instructed him to have some good food for lunch from nearby. He said, "Listen, Raqib, you had to finish breakfast hurriedly because of me. Now that both of us will be inside the movie theater, please have your meal at your leisure."

After that, he and Tilottama went inside the theater. Raktim requested Tilottama to click a few snaps of him beside a life-size cut-out of the famous film director Rituporno Ghosh. Since Rituporno had directed the critically acclaimed movie *Raincoat*, based on O. Henry's short story, 'The Gift of the Magi,' Raktim had become an ardent follower of his works. Though they went to sit in the corner seats of the row, both of them noticed that the hall was mostly empty. The movie for which Tilottama had bought tickets was by a new director making his first art film. So, in this era of OTT platforms, there were few takers for such a work.

When the cinema finally started, Raktim got them two big buckets of popcorn. But the darkness of the theater hall and their closeness soon made them forget the popcorn, as their lips melted into each other's arms. With their eyes closed, they were no longer watching anything on the screen.

Chapter 29

Mohor Kunj was about four kilometers away from Priya Cinema Hall. After spending a couple of hours in the cinema hall, Raktim and Tilottama went there, sitting silently with their hands in each other's. The calmness of the moment felt unnatural. The silence between them was speaking relentlessly, though both sat mute. The atmosphere suddenly felt heavy. Then Tilottama broke the hush and asked, "Hey, Raktim! Tell me clearly, what do you truly want?"

Hearing the question, Raktim felt an unsaid sorrow crashing against the limits of his tolerance like wave after wave. He could hardly control his emotions anymore and broke down. With tearful eyes, he confessed, "All of us are actually victims of circumstances. Although you have the option to live the rest of your life with a person you love, I hardly have such an option. There is no chance for me, at least in this life."

"No, Raktim, no... we shouldn't let that happen. You should marry a good girl and build a family. You, too, have to live your life."

"Tilottama, I stopped thinking about myself a long time ago. My only goal now is to see you happy and settled, to see you live your dreams. And that's why I must move away from your life as soon as possible."

Chapter 30

The exams were over for the schoolchildren, so there was a lot of pending work on the answer sheets to be corrected. Raktim barely had three days in hand to finish his job. But such tasks require a settled frame of mind, which he presently did not possess, as he could hardly control his restless thoughts. He had never been prepared for such a state, though he knew that a good and healthy life always requires a sound state of mind. Even a few years ago, people did not give much importance to mental well-being, but now they are far more aware of how to control their minds to lead a healthier life.

Raktim and Tilottama went to a shopping mall. While Tilottama was busy selecting some clothes to gift him, Raktim kept thinking about those standing just a few steps away. Soon, Tilottama brought a nice-looking shirt and said, "Quickly go to the trial room and put this on to check."

Raktim obliged like an obedient boy and returned after trying it on. Tilottama stood there, a question in her eyes, and her mask slightly lowered. Without wasting time, Raktim replied, "I like it very much, really."

Tilottama proudly said, "Well, next time, wear this shirt to meet me. I would love that."

Raktim nodded. "So be it. But for now, I think we should move towards the food court to have something."

While eating, Raktim clicked some candid photographs of Tilottama on his phone. After finishing the food, Tilottama said, "Now we will visit BBC Park to spend some time there. After that, you will drop me off at my home and then go back to Suri. After reaching home, don't forget to send me a text message about your arrival."

Hearing this, Raktim checked his phone and saw that BBC Park in Patuli was about seven kilometres from South City Mall, and it would take them about twenty minutes to reach there by car. It was then that he remembered Arghya lived in Patuli. Arghya and Priyanka had invited him to their place quite a few times, but he had never been able to go.

Upon reaching BBC Park, they found couples busy romancing each other at various spots. A few were doing so in quite a disturbing way by the water pool in the park. Raktim and Tilottama smilingly walked past all these, holding each other's hands. They chose a comparatively lonely place by the water to sit close to each other. Raktim even clicked a few photographs of them together. Then he hugged Tilottama lightly and reminded her, "In a few months, your life will change. There will be new people around. Please try to keep me in your mind amidst them. It's completely up to you whether you will remember me in the future or not, but believe me, the time we have spent together so far will never become a lie, and this moment—sitting together by the flowing water at BBC Park—will never become a lie. These are our personal times together."

Raktim paused after speaking for so long. Tilottama answered, "No, Raktim, I can never deny the times we have spent together. I will remember them forever."

Raktim probably would have said something more, but Tilottama's lips stopped him by pressing against his. He started flowing again, perhaps for the last time. Both of them felt that life held no separation and no mourning for them. There was no end to anything between them. An emotional darkness prevailed around them.

Chapter 31

Raktim still felt torn between the thought that emotion interferes first in one's romantic life, and the belief that a person draws in emotion by force in the middle of romance and then gets lost in it. Undeniably, love brings new habits into one's life. But when such habits persist even after love disappears with the course of time, one faces the real turmoil of life. For example, in those days, when no phone calls came from Tilottama in the late hours of the night, Raktim felt deeply troubled. Durga Puja came and went, and the twenty-second of December was approaching. Raktim struggled, yet he resisted making frequent calls to Tilottama. Tilottama, too, maintained very little contact. An unexplained disappointment took over Raktim's mind, as if a script had gone awry.

He surrendered to the troubles of life to the point where he began refusing requests from top publishers for new manuscripts. He explained his condition to the world as a psychological state called writer's block. In silence, he kept checking Tilottama's WhatsApp status, watching her photographs of wedding shopping alongside her groom-to-be, Samarpan, having lunch together, or devouring pre-wedding feasts at relatives' places. Those snaps pierced his soul with pain, yet he ensured nobody heard his cry.

Finding no other way, he stared blankly at Tilottama's Truecaller notifications till late at night, when for hours it showed the status "On a call," until he unknowingly fell asleep. Walking through a crossword puzzle called life, Raktim smoked at least a pack of cigarettes every night. He refrained from looking back at his past, where beautiful memories with Tilottama would have left him bloodied. Raktim felt that someone had robbed him of melodies, rhythms, and the waves of happiness that once buoyed him to write beautiful poetry.

Chapter 32

After his grandmother passed away, Raktim once found a handwritten note of hers in which she had written, "Whoever leaves, leaves to never come again. Only memories remain to pierce you with pain." The sentences could have ended with ellipses, but such punctuation marks were not common in those days. That day, on their way back from BBC Park, Tilottama had rested her head on his left shoulder and fallen asleep from tiredness. Raktim remembered how he had caressed her hair, which had fallen over her forehead, and how he had taken off the black bindi she wore.

Raktim's love for Tilottama was always selfless. So he kept her bindi as a token of memory that he would treasure for the rest of his life.

After trying to watch a few inspirational videos on social media, Raktim felt very disappointed and stopped watching them altogether. Everything appeared hollow and meaningless. He began to understand that only he could find the solution to his condition. Meanwhile, his favorite poet had also called him at least a dozen times, but Raktim had no wish to talk. Ayantika had sent a voice message, but he had not opened it yet.

When Tapas Uncle delivered the newspapers, as he did every day, Biswanath Babu called Raktim and asked, "Why do you remain so forgetful these days? Did something happen?"

Malati Devi echoed the concern: "I find you travelling to Kolkata frequently nowadays. I hope you are not facing any trouble there. After all, the situation everywhere is so grim!"

Near Suri Hospital, Dr. Bishnu Bhattacharya stayed in his chamber at Pamela Pharmacy till ten at night. He was a specialist in neurology and psychiatry. Finding no respite, Raktim visited him. The doctor examined him carefully, conducted some tests, prescribed a few medicines, and then advised, "See, you are young, so do not look away from the positives of life. If you lose hope, you actually damage your health."

While coming out of the doctor's chamber, Raktim noticed a girl sitting there, absorbed in her mobile phone. He quietly walked past her in a hurry and told himself, "Thank God! Lisa didn't notice me."

Chapter 33

In between all this, one day, Tilottama sent a very short message on WhatsApp, saying that relatives were almost pouring into their house every day to celebrate the upcoming marriage. Raktim saw the message but managed to mince words in his reply. Time flew by, and soon it was the fourteenth of December. Raktim could not resist himself anymore and wrote, "How are you? Is everything going well?" The reply came almost two hours later, in which Tilottama said that she had been forced to take two months' leave from the office for her marriage and that, before leaving, she would attend the office for the last time the following day.

Raktim kept playing her voice message. He went crazy after finally hearing her voice after a long while.

He had no more than three thousand bucks in his pocket, including cash and online wallet funds. A few days ago, he had lent around ten thousand rupees to Bivash, but even after repeatedly pressing him over calls and messages, Bivash had not returned the money. Raktim felt bad because he did not like people who failed to keep their promises about money.

That day, Raktim remained immersed in the deepest thoughts of his life. It was his last chance to meet Tilottama, talk to her, touch her before she got married off to someone else. He did not want to lose it while sitting idle. He thought that, though it would be a risk, he should go to meet her. So he quickly called and booked Raqib for 2,500 rupees to take him to Kolkata, knowing well that it was just half the amount he would actually have to pay Raqib for the travel. Without a second thought, he packed his bag and got ready.

"*Bhaijan*, I'm feeling very hungry now!" Raqib's words stung Raktim, who had just a single five-hundred-rupee note left in his pocket. They had already traveled a long way without food. Raktim did not even buy his cigarettes. Ignoring the poor lad's request and completely forgetting to check his phone for the GPS location, Raktim lay his tired and hungry body in the backseat of the car and murmured, "How far is Garia?"

Then he could not resist himself and called Tilottama. After a couple of failed attempts, she finally answered.

"Yes! Tell me."

"Where are you?"

"I'm at the office and about to leave in a while. But why are you asking?"

"I'm waiting for you in the car at the nearby crossing. One last time, I would like to travel with you to Madhyamgram."

"Are you crazy, Raktim! I'm about to get married in a week from now, so please don't act childishly!"

"Please, Tilottama, please try to understand my situation too!"

"Alright. You wait there. Give me some time to wrap up my office work. But I can't go with you to Madhyamgram. I have to go to one of my relatives' places in Kasba now. From there, Samarpan and I will travel together to Madhyamgram."

"Why Samarpan?"

Tilottama paused for a while before answering, "At Kasba, there is a tour and travel company known to Samarpan. We will go there together to book our honeymoon trip to Goa."

A visibly disappointed Raktim suddenly realized that a losing lover lives through stronger pain than Jesus.

Burning in the last sunrays of the dusk, Raktim only managed to utter, "Fine. I'm waiting."

Chapter 34

The Garia crossing was bathed in the day-end sunlight, and the traffic whisked past the busy crowd jostling around as they did every day, all completely unaware of a small-town young man who stood among them, lost in eternal darkness as the last ray of hope inside him had just gone out. Raktim would never let anyone know that. Then, suddenly, Tilottama walked up to him one last time, her face covered with a mask.

Raktim opened the car door to let Tilottama in, and then followed her to the back seat. After setting the Google location for the Kasba address, when Raqib started the car, Raktim quickly added, "Raqib, can you drive slowly, please—I mean, really slow." Then he turned toward Tilottama and silently passed her a large pack of dark chocolate. She took it, carefully tucked it into her back pocket, and then said, "Raqib, please play the FM radio."

"Sure, sister," Raqib replied, tuning to a soft romantic number at a low volume. Tilottama moved closer to Raktim, looked directly into his eyes, and said slowly, "Look, Raktim, next week on this very day, I'm going to get hitched with Samarpan. So I think you know well what risk I took today to come and meet you."

Raktim's eyes filled with tears. He searched for words but failed, so he held her hands in his lap and sat silently, lost in the thought of their separation. Tilottama gave him some time before saying, "We live only once, Raktim. So it's important to live it well." In a trembling voice, Raktim managed to tell Raqib, "Raqib, slow down, please... can't you?" Then he pressed Tilottama's hands tighter and continued, "Will you remember the time we spent together, even after a decade from now? Will you remember me then? Assure me you won't forget anything." Raktim wept. There was nothing more he could say.

"Just a decade of remembrance—is that what you're asking for? Dear, I will remember the time we spent together until my last breath. Take my word."

Raktim was struggling for words when Tilottama suddenly asked Raqib to stop the car before a sweet shop. She then turned to Raktim and said, "I shouldn't visit a relative's place empty-handed, especially when I'm going there after such a long time. So I must buy some sweets. Can you wait in the car while I get them?" Raktim stopped her and quickly took out his wallet, fished out the only two-hundred-rupee note he had left, and handed it to her with a smile. "Let me do the honor of buying them."

When she returned from the sweet shop, standing outside the car door, Tilottama held out a pack of sweets toward him and said, "These sweets are for you, Raktim." Raktim silently accepted her gift and looked at her blankly. She spoke again, "My relative's house is only a few steps from here, so I'll walk the rest of the way." She paused and added, "You are a good man, Raktim. Stay well." With that, she closed the car door.

From the moving car, Raktim watched Tilottama's figure until it vanished into the crowd ahead. He realized that their early-December separation had scripted an entire winter of loneliness for him. He felt he should quit writing—leave the world of literature altogether. He could find no light ahead; only a hollow path of eternal darkness lay before him. Keeping his hand on the empty seat beside him, Raktim whispered, "Take me to Patuli."

Chapter 35

At least three months had passed since the calendar page had turned from 2022 to 2023. Raktim's bond with Youth Novel Prize winner Hiralal Mandal had recently grown stronger; they had almost become brothers-in-arms. Raktim wore the glasses and the shirt he had received as gifts from Tilottama. He hesitated a bit before entering through the glass door of the coffee shop. But as he stepped into the cool, conditioned air inside, it blew him away. It was a half-empty café, and there, in a pre-booked seat in the corner, sat Tilottama. This was the first time Raktim had seen the married avatar of Tilottama, and his heart stopped for a moment. She was in a neatly worn saree, with vermillion smeared on the parting of her carefully done hair. There were *sankha-polas* on her hands. She had become healthier, and perhaps even fairer. The Tilottama who once walked through College Street and roamed the Book Fair hand in hand with Raktim was no more. She had become a newlywed bride.

Raktim looked at her, shilly-shally. The one who could have become his wife was now somebody else's wife, after all.

At last, Tilottama placed her kohl-smeared eyes upon Raktim, and Raktim looked back. Perhaps ages flew by. A river full of water flowed from the source to the sea. A light-year stopped flowing. But time never stops. Searching for words, Raktim dragged his feet until Tilottama finally spoke, "Sit here. How are you?"

A spell of silence followed, for Raktim felt it was a really tough question to answer—because, for a long while, he had never asked himself that. But he eventually found his footing, gathered a touch of indifference in his voice and nonchalance in his smile, and said, "Well, all good. What about you?"

Tilottama did not answer. She looked away. Was she afraid of looking at Raktim? Was she hesitant about something? Was she afraid of being caught red-handed? But how? Why? Was there any trace of melancholy lurking behind the manicured marriage Tilottama was trying to hide? Was this the life she truly wanted to live? Or had she not wanted to begin a life by leaving Raktim in the dark? Were the three of them living three different lives? Were there truths that Tilottama was desperately trying to conceal?

The thoughts kept Raktim from being mindful until the waiter dressed in white came and asked for the order: "Sir, what will you have?"

Raktim smiled lightly, "Black coffee."

Tilottama smiled back and nodded.

Raktim took out his credit card from his wallet and handed it to the waiter. His wallet was familiar to her. As the waiter left, Raktim took out his little magazine from the grey side bag and said, "*Stories of Poetry*—this is your courtesy copy. Your poem, *Aharan*, or *Riding*, is published."

Raktim paused. Then he took out another book from his grey side bag. Looking directly into Tilottama's eyes, he said, "Tilottama, you left my life forever, but my writings never left me. So I embraced them with open arms, and I intend to live with each other's pain for the rest of my life. Tilottama, this is my first novel. I will be happy if you read it."

As he had been packing the book in gift wrap for Tilottama, the waiter returned with two cups of black coffee, the credit card, and the printed bill. Taking the bill from him, Raktim looked back at Tilottama and shrugged, "I'm in real hurry today, so I can't have coffee with you. In a few moments, there will be a book inauguration ceremony at the Mahabodhi Society, and I have to be on time. I wanted this book to touch your hands before it reached my readers. My wish is fulfilled. Perhaps we will meet again. See you till then."

While leaving, Raktim felt his feet grow heavy, but he dragged himself like a piece of stone. Silently, he walked out of the coffee shop to the cab waiting outside.

Spellbound in a different world of silence, Tilottama watched how, amidst the darkness of the ever-bustling city, their romance was fading frame by frame—their beautiful evenings at College Square once cladded in Book Fair dust, their cozy dark-corner seat cuddling at Priya Cinema Hall, their golden dusk hours spent at Mohor Kunj, the meetings at Patuli Bus Stop, the waiting by the Dhalai Bridge—each and every memory was fading.

The coffee had gone cold by then. Unmindfully opening the wrapping paper, Tilottama discovered the novel titled *Yet Life!* She quickly turned a few pages and found a paragraph: "To the person to whom I have dedicated all my writings, not just this book—To Tilottama!"

Tilottama could not hold her tears; they rained like an untimed monsoon.

In the coffee shop, a song was playing:

Tomake bujhina priyo, bujho na tumi amay / Duratto bare; jogajog nibhe jai

(Neither do I understand you, nor do you understand me / The distance keeps widening, and the contact fades.)

Quickly, she looked at her watch, her eyes teary. It had just ticked seven.